Samuel Chessman

Leach family record

Descendants of Lawrence Leach of Salem

Samuel Chessman

Leach family record
Descendants of Lawrence Leach of Salem

ISBN/EAN: 9783337210281

Printed in Europe, USA, Canada, Australia, Japan

Cover: Foto ©Raphael Reischuk / pixelio.de

More available books at **www.hansebooks.com**

Leach Family Record.

DESCENDANTS OF

LAWRENCE LEACH

OF

Salem, Mass., 1629.

THROUGH HIS SON GILES, OF BRIDGEWATER, MASS., 1665.

COMPILED BY

SAMUEL CHESSMAN.

ALBANY, N. Y.:
JOEL MUNSELL'S SONS, PUBLISHERS.
1898.

HOME AT MERRIMACK, HILLSBORO COUNTY, N. H.,

Of Mehitable Leach (No. 180, b. 1785), wife of Samuel Chesman, where they lived from 1816 to 1828, near Reed's Ferry, ten miles below the city of Manchester, on the Merrimack river.

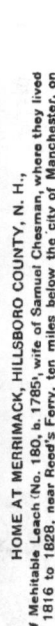

MEHITABLE LEACH.
No. 180.

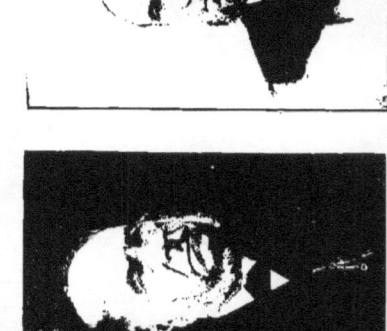

ROBT. CHESMAN.

SAMUEL CHESMAN.
No. 208.

JULIA A. OTTERSON,
No. 207.

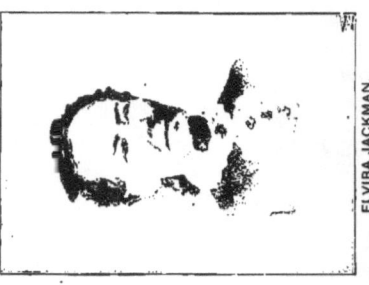

ELVIRA JACKMAN.
No. 206.

HISTORICAL RECORDS OF THE LEACH FAMILY, TAKEN FROM PUBLIC AND PRIVATE RECORDS.

——— .. - -

The first item below is from Josiah Granville Leach, in a printed slip sent to different members of the family:

"Lawrence Leach, who, with his wife Elizabeth and sons John, Richard and Robert, came from England to Salem, Mass., in 1629, where he continued to live until his death in 1662, aged 83 years. From researches made I am led to believe his descendants number over 10,000. One of the most numerous branches of his posterity is that descended from his son Giles Leach, who was born at Salem, Mass., and married Ann Nokes at Weymouth, 1656, and settled in Bridgewater in 1664, where he became entitled by purchase to one fifty-sixth share of the thousands of acres of land bought in 1645 of the old Indian chief Massasoit (King Philip's father) by Miles Standish, Samuel Hash and Constant Southworth for the use of the fifty-six original proprietors. When Lawrence Leach was about leaving old England for New England, Governor John Winthrop, who had not then come to America, wrote from Gravesend, England, under date of April 17, 1629, a long letter concerning the new colony to Governor John Endicott, of Massachusetts Bay Colony, in which letter he wrote the following: 'We desire you to take notice of one Lawrence Leach, whom we have found a careful and painsful man and we doubt not he will continue his diligence.'"

His life in America would seem to have fully justified the confidence reposed in him by Governor Winthrop. It is recorded in one of the histories of Massachusetts, a sketch of him which contains the following: "Lawrence Leach held many important offices and the usefulness of his life gained respect for his memory."

Mr. J. G. Leach says, as a matter of further interest: "Let me state that some years ago my cousin, William Sanford Leach, son of Elbridge Gerry Leach, of Boston, made the English ancestry of our family a matter of research, and it is said he traced the family back to John Leach, surgeon to King Edward the Third. My cousin died in the Union army, and the data he made has been lost."

The coat of arms of the family has upon it three crowns, and the significance of these crowns is said to be this: that on one occasion while the kings of France and Scotland were prisoners of King Edward, the three kings dined at the house of John Leach and, as a token of the incident, on leaving King Edward handed to Leach three crowns. Afterwards, when the king granted him a large landed estate, three crowns were placed on his arms.

The following is the history of the Leach family that descended from Giles Leach (son of Lawrence Leach, of Salem, Mass.), who settled in West Bridgewater before

1665, married Anne Nokes, of Weymouth, 1656. She lived in Deacon Bass' family, Braintree. Mitchel's history of Bridgewater says there was born to them the following named children, and perhaps others:

1. Sarah Leach, b. in 1656.
2. Elizabeth Leach, b. in 1662.
3. Samuel Leach, b. 1662.
4. David Leach.
5. John Leach.
6. Ebenezer Leach.
7. Benjamin Leach.

Sarah Leach (1) m. John Aldrich. Elizabeth Leach (2) m. John Emerson, 1693. Sarah and Samuel b. at Weymouth.

SAMUEL LEACH (3), son of Giles and Anne Nokes Leach, m. Mary, dau. of Nicholas Byram. Children:

8. Samuel Leach.
9. Josiah Leach.
10. Seth Leach.
11. Elijah Leach.

DAVID LEACH (4), son of Giles and Anne Nokes Leach, m. Hannah ————. Children:

12. Mercy Leach, b. 1693.
13. Hannah Leach, b. 1696; d. young.
14. Ephraim Leach, b. 1699.
15. Experience Leach, b. 1702.
16. David Leach, b. 1706.

17. Mehitabel Leach, b. 1711.
18. Abigail Leach, b. 1714.

David Leach (4) d. 1757; widow Hannah then m. Ebenezer Edson in 1758.

JOHN LEACH (5), son of Giles and Anne Nokes Leach, m. Alice. Children:

19. John Leach, b. 1695.
20. Giles Leach, b. 1697.
21. Stephen Leach, b. 1698.
22. Alice Leach, b. 1700.
23. Ebenezer Leach, b. 1702.
24. Mehitabel Leach, b. 1704.
25. Timothy Leach, b. 1707.
26. Nehemiah Leach, b. 1709.
27. Solomon Leach, b. 1712.
28. Jesse Leach, b. 1714; d. 1744.

EBENEZER LEACH (6), son of Giles and Anne Nokes Leach, m. Prudence Stetson, of Scituate, in 1707. One child:

29. Lydia Leach, who m. Ephraim Jackson.

BENJAMIN LEACH (7), son of Giles and Anne Nokes Leach, m. Hepzibah Washburn, 1702. Children:

30. Ann Leach, b. 1703.
31. Joseph Leach, b. 1705.
32. Mary Leach, b. 1708.
33. Sarah Leach, b. 1711.

34. Benjamin Leach, b. 1713.
35. Ichabod Leach, b. 1716; d. yonng.
36. Jerethmeal Leach, b. 1718 } twins.
37. Benanuel Leach, b. 1718 }
38. Nokes Leach, b. 1720.
39. Susanna Leach, b. 1722.
40. Hannah Leach, b. 1725.
41. Phebe Leach, m. Abner Forbes.
42. Nathan Leach.
43. Eunice Leach.

Sarah Leach (33) m. Timothy Leach, 1732.
Susanna Leach (39) m. Ezra Washburn, 1742.

SAMUEL LEACH (8), son of Samuel and Mary
Byram Leach, m. Content ———. Children:

45. Elijah Leach, b. 1726.
46. Samuel Leach, d. about 1756.

SETH LEACH (10), son of Samuel and Mary Byram
Leach, m. dau. of Thomas Whitman. One son:

47. Seth Leach, who had a son, Thomas, who was probably the father of Caleb Leach, formerly of Plymouth, a clock maker and mechanic.

Seth Leach (47) m. June, dau. of Joseph Harvey, 1732.

ELIJAH LEACH (11), son of Samuel and Mary
Byram Leach, m. Jemima, dau. of Benjamin Snow, 1745.
Children:

48. Elijah Leach, b. 1746.
49. Jemima Leach, b. 1749.

Elijah Leach (11) removed to Westmoreland; d. 1763.
Elijah Leach (48) m. Ruth Prince, of Kingston, 1764.
Jemima Leach (49) m. James Loven, 1785.

JOHN LEACH (19), son of John and Alice Leach, m.
Susanna White, 1719. Children:

50. Alice Leach, who m. David Perkins, 1738.
51. Abijah Leach.
52. Stephen Leach, d. before his father.

GILES LEACH (20) went to Halifax; m., and had
children:

53. Mirah Leach, b. 1734.
54. Elizabeth Leach, and probably others.
55. John Leach. He had a son, John Mirah Leach (53),
was the father of
57. Silvanus Leach.

Elizabeth (54) m. Jonah Shutliff, of Maine.

STEPHEN LEACH (52), son of John and Susanna
White Leach, m. dau. of John Hooper, 1725. Children:

58. Ann Leach, b. 1727.
59. Stephen Leach, b. 1730; his widow m. Ebenezer
Snow, 1737.

EBENEZER LEACH, son of John and Alice Leach,
m. Joanna, dau. of Josiah Washburn, 1734. Children:

60. Daniel Leach, b. 1735.
61. Joanna Leach, b. 1738.

Mitchel says he m. Lydia Tilson, 1739, and Deborah
Sampson, 1751; he d. 1753.

Ebenezer Leach m. Mary Wilbor, 1741.

Deborah Leach m. Nathan Leach, 1771.

Eben Leach d. 1803, very aged.

TIMOTHY LEACH (25), son of John and Alice Leach,
m. Sarah, dau. of Benjamin Leach, 1732. Children:

62. Rebecca Leach, b. 1733.
63. Ichabod Leach, b. 1735.
64. Sarah Leach, b. 1739.
65. Jonathan Leach, b. 1741.
66. Levi Leach, b. 1744.
67. Nathan Leach, b. 1746.
68. Anne Leach, b. 1749.
69. Timothy Leach, b. 1751.

Rebecca Leach (62) m. Joshua Warren, Jr., 1760.

Sarah Leach (64) m. Jona Hayward, of E., 1762.

Anne Leach (68) m. James Sturtevant, 1769.

NEHEMIAH LEACH (26), son of John and Alice
Leach, m. Mary Stapels. Children:

70. Abigail Leach, b. 1730.
71. Mercy Leach, b. 1732.

Second wife, a Bryant, of Plymouth.

72. James Leach, b. 1737.
73. Ruth Leach, b. 1739.
74. Robert Leach, b. 1740.

75. Huldah Leach, b. 1742.
76. Mehitabel Leach, b. 1744.
77. Lydia Leach.
78. Nehemiah Leach.
79. Caleb Leach.
80. Susanna Leach.

Nehemiah Leach (26), d. 1769; wife d. 1775.
Abigail Leach (70), m. Benjamin Keith, 1749.
Mercy Leach (71), m. Nathan Latham, 1756.
Ruth Leach (73), m. Benjamin Packard, 1762.
Huldah Leach (75), m. Daniel Lazell, 1761.
Mehitable Leach (76), m. Nathan Jones.
Lydia Leach (77), m. John Dickerman, 1770.
Susanna Leach (80), m. Deacon Isaac Wilbor.

SOLOMON LEACH (27), son of John and Alice
Leach, m. Tabitha, dau. of Samuel Washburn, 1736. She
d. 1736. He m. Jerusha Bryant, of Plympton, 1739.
Child:

81. Abisha Leach, b. 1739.

Second wife d. 1743. He m. Hannah Leach (40) in
1840. Children:

82. Jerusha Leach, b. 1746.
83. Solomon Leach, b. 1750.
84. Israel Leach, b. 1752.
85. Hannah Leach, b. 1755.
86. Susanna Leach, b. 1758.
87. Joseph Leach, b. 1760.

Jerusha Leach (82) m. Isaac Leach, of Westmoreland, 1793.

Abisha Leach (81) lived in Easton, and was the father of

88. Joshua Leach.
89. Philip Leach, was a lawyer in Maine.
90. Shepard Leach.

JESSE LEACH (28), son of John and Alice Leach, m. Alice Churchill. Tradition says she was a very beautiful woman. Children:

91. Lodock Leach, b. 1741.
92. Giles Leach, b.
93. Alice Leach.
94. Calvin Leach.

Jesse Leach (28) d. 1744. His widow m. Daniel Bacon, 1772.

Alice Leach (93) m. Silas Leach, 1778.

JAMES LEACH (parentage unknown). He and his wife lived in Kingston. Children:

95. Elizabeth Leach, b. 1735.
96. Mercy Leach, b. 1738.
97. Sarah Leach, b. 1740.

DEACON JOSEPH LEACH (31), son of Benjamin and Hepzibah Washburn Leach, m. Ann Harris, 1736. Children:

98. Benjamin Leach.

99. Japthah Leach.
100. Isaiah Leach.

BENJAMIN LEACH (34), son of Benjamin and Hepzibah Washburn Leach, m. Hannah, dau. of John Keith,
1740. Children:

101. Jedediah Leach.
102. Peleg Leach.
103. Benjamin Leach.
104. Eliphlet Leach.

Benjamin Leach (103) m. Joanna Wilbor, 1751. Benjamin Leach m. widow Abigail Bassett, 1763. Widow
Hannah m. Israel Washburn, and afterwards m. Dea. Hall,
of Raynham.

Benanuel Leach (37) son of Benjamin and Hepzibah
Leach, m. Betty Perkins, 1741, and Elizabeth, dau. of
Samuel Edson, 1745. Benanuel Leach m. Mehitabel,
dau. of Benj. Allen, of E. B.

SAMUEL LEACH (46), son of Samuel and Content
Leach, m. Phebe ———. Children:

105. Phebe Leach, b. 1753.
106. Silas Leach, b. 1755.
107. Samuel Leach, b. 1757.
108. Jeshurun Leach, b. 1760.

He died in the army, 1760, aged 33 years.

Silas Leach (106), son of Samuel and Phebe Leach, m.
Alice Leach (93) in 1778.

Samuel Leach (107) went to New York.

STEPHEN LEACH (52). son of John and Susana White Leach, m. Lydia Flora, of Halifax, 1745. Children:

109. Lemuel Leach, b. 1745.
110. Stephen Leach, b. 1747.
111. Jeremiah Leach, b. 1751.

Stephen Leach (52) m. Sarah, dau. of Thomas Hooper, 1749. Stephen Leach, in 1756, belonged to the Baptist Church in Swanzey.

CAPT. SIMON LEACH. son of Giles (20), settled in St. Corner; m. Elizabeth, dau. of Theophilus Curtis, 1765. Children:

112. Lot Leach.
113. Relief Leach.
114. Vashti Leach.

Capt. Simon Leach d. 1777, aged 43 years.
Relief Leach (113) m. Oliver Harris, 1789.
Vashti Leach (114) m. William Harris, 1796.

DEA. DANIEL LEACH (60), son of Ebenezer and Joanna Washburn Leach, m. Bethia, dau. of Samuel Keith, 1760. Children:

115. Joanna Leach, b. 1761.
116. Bethiah Leach, b. 1764.
117. Deborah Leach, b. 1766.
118. Ebenezer Leach, b. 1768.
119. Daniel Leach, b. 1771.
120. Olive Leach, b. 1773.

121. Lydia Leach, b. 1775.
122. Susanna Leach, b. 1778.
123. Celia Leach, b. 1780.

Joannah Leach (115) m. dau. of Isaac Wilbor.
Deborah Leach (117) m. Perez White, 1778.
Olive Leach (120) m. Keziah Fobes, 1793.
Susanna Leach (122) m. Isaac Hooper, 1805.
Celia Leach (123) m. Eliab Hayward, 1803.

ICHABOD LEACH (63). son of Timothy and Sarah Leach. m. Penelope Cobb, 1790. Children:

124. Jerathmeal Leach.
125. Ephraim Leach.
126. Bakus Leach.
127. Abigail Leach.

Jeruthmuel Leach (124) m. Clarisa Leach, 1789, and went to Warren.

Ephraim Leach (125) m. Sarah, dau. of Zenas Conant, 1805.

Bakus Leach (126) m. Bethiah Hayward, 1804.

Abigail Leach (127) m. Freeman Jones, 1792.

JONATHAN LEACH (65), or Jonathan, son of William Leach, m. Experience Hartwell, 1768. Children:

128. Silence Leach, b. 1768.
129. Olive Leach, b. 1770.
130. Lois Leach, b. 1772.
131. Eunice Leach, b. 1772.

Jonathan Leach. parentage not known.

LEVI LEACH (66), m. Hannah, dau. of Abner Forbes, 1771. One son:

132. Levi Leach.

NATHAN LEACH (67), son of Timothy and Sarah Leach, lived in N. B.; m. Deborah, dau. of William Leach, or perhaps widow of Ebenezer Leach. 1771. Children:

133. Reliance Leach, b. May 29, 1772.
134. Thaddeus Leach, b. March 13, 1775.
135. Oliver Leach, m. Sally Brown, 1803.
136. Sarah Leach, m. Allen Smith, 1815.
137. Libbeus Leach.
138. Eliphelet Leach, m. Hannah Show, Dec. 11. 1806.
139. Nathan Leach, m. Mehitabel Gloyd, 1805.

The father d. Feb. 1, 1826, aged 79. Mother d. Jan. 14, 1834, aged 83.

OLIVER LEACH (135). m. Sally. dau. of Knight Brown, 1803. Children:

140. Elbrige Leach, m. Deborah H. Joslyn, of Hanover.
141. John Leach, m. Lydia French.
142. Oliver Leach. m. Susanna Howland. Oct. 27, 1828.
143. Aaron Leach, shot while gunning. May 13. 1821.
144. Allen Leach, m. Lydia Jenkins.
145. Sarah Leach.

The wife d. May 15, 1816, aged 34. He then m. Mary, dau. of Peleg Stetson, 1817. Children:

146. Marcus Leach, b. Dec. 7, 1818; m. Eliza P. Bourne, of Hanson, Oct. 24, 1847.

147. Calvin Stetson Leach, d. Jan. 15, 1842, aged 22.
148. Aaron Davis Leach, m. Sophia Worth.
149. Emily Jane Leach.
150. Lucius Leach, m. Celia Howland, March 7, 1855.
151. Peleg Stetson Leach, m., 1st, Angeline Damon,
     Feb. 9, 1854; 2d, Eliza D. Packard, Dec. 31,
     1863.
152. Charlotte Eveline Leach, m. Daniel Hall.
153. Maria Augusta Leach.
154. Levi Leach, m. Sylvia D. Cook, Oct. 4, 1861.

JAMES LEACH (72), son of Nehemiah and Mary
Staples Leach, m. Huldah, dau. of Robert Keith, 1765.
Children:

155. Alpheus Leach.
156. Apollas Leach.
157. Caleb Leach.
158. James Leach.
159. Chloe Leach.
160. Roxiliana Leach.
161. Mercy Leach.
162. Sarah Leach.
163. Huldah Leach.
164. Ruth Leach.

James Leach (158), son of James and Huldah Keith
Leach, m. Betsey, dau. of Nathaniel Leonard, of Taunton,
1811.

Chloe Leach (159), m. Col. Solomon Forbes, 1807.

Roxiliana Leach (160), m. Elias Dunbar, 1799.

Mercy Leach (161). m. Abraham Gould. 1809.
Sarah Leach (162), m. Jonathan Keith, 1792.
Huldah Leach (163), m. George Chipman, 1803.
Ruth Leach (164), m. Joseph Bassett, 1792.

NEHEMIAH LEACH (78), son of Nehemiah and
Mary Staples Leach, m. Constant, dau. of Robert Keith,
1772. Children:

   165. Eliphelet Leach.

   166. Oliver Leach.

   167. Lewis Leach and others.

Eliphlet Leach (165) m. Phebe Caswell, 1798.

CALEB LEACH (79), m. Molly Adams, 1780. One
daughter:

   168. Lydia Leach, b. 1782.

ZADOCK LEACH (91). son of Jesse and Alice
Churchill Leach, m. Susanna, dau. of Ezra Washburn, of
M., 1763. Children:

   169. Susanna Leach.

   170. Bozer Leach.

   171. Abraham Leach.

   172. Zebedee Leach.

   173. Parnel Leach, m. Apollos Eaton, of M., 1795.

   174. Rufus Leach.

   175. Zadock Leach.

Susanna Leach (169). m. Edward Richmond, 1788.

Rufus Leach (174) m. Nancy. dau. of Ebenezer Perkins.
1798. and went to New York.

2

GILES LEACH (92), son of Jesse and Alice Churchill Leach, m. Mehitabel Wilbur, dau. of Meshack and Elizabeth Wilbur, of Raynham, March 12, 1777. Children:

176. Chloe Leach, b. March 17, 1778.
177. Solomon Leach, b. Nov. 7, 1779.
178. Alice Leach, b. June 25, 1781; d. April 1, 1811.
179. Hosea Leach, b. March 5, 1783.
180. Mehitabel Leach, b. April 24, 1785.
181. Giles Leach, b. May 27, 1787; d. Feb., 1791.
182. Abigail Leach, b. July 31, 1789.
183. Kisiah Leach, b. Aug. 2, 1791; d. 1823.
184. Laura Leach, b. Aug. 11, 1793.
185. Betsey Leach, b. Oct. 25, 1795.
186. One child, still-born March 19, 1798.
187. Giles Leach, b. Jan. 31, 1799.

Giles Leach (92), the father, d. June 31, 1799, aged about 56 years.

His widow, Mehitabel, m. Luther Hull, of Raynham, 1806. He died. She died.

The above record of Giles Leach's (92) family does not agree with Mitchel. He omits 183, and other errors are found in his record of the family. The above is a correct copy from Samuel Chesman's bible (husband of 180).

CHLOE LEACH (176), dau. of Giles and Mehitabel Wilbur Leach, m. Zephaniah Wilbur, of Raynham, Mass., 1796. Children:

188. Franklin Wilbur, b. 1799; m. Betsey Dean.
189. Solomon Wilbur.

190. Charlotte Wilbur, m. John Eddy.
191. Abigail Wilbur, m. David Clark.
192. Zephaniah Wilbur. m. Prissila Ashley.
193. Daniel Wilbur, m. Fanny Ashley.

SOLOMON LEACH (177) m. Mary Holmes. of K., in 1806, and went to Rochester or Mattaposit. I think my mother told me they had several sons, but from other sources I have been informed that they had only one child, a daughter. — S. C.

ALICE LEACH (178), m. Seth Crossman. 1804. Children:

194. Melvin Crossman, date not known; he d. in Pittsburg, Pa., about 1830, unmarried. This was told to me by one, John Morrow, who was acquainted with him. — S. C.
195. Seth Crossman learned the nailers' trade of Uncle Lewis Bartlett at the same time that I did; he went west, I think, to Cleveland, Ohio, and married. Had children:
196. Valeria Crossman, m. Leonard Mitchel, of Wareham. She d. about 1829. One or two children. She died of measles. I was present when she died. Mitchel then m. Miss Snow, a sister of the little dwarf Snow.

HOSEA LEACH (179), m. Hannah, dau. of Capt. Seth Keith, 1808. Children:

197. Mary Ann Leach, b. Sept. 26, 1808.

198. Lambert Leach, b. April 29, 1810.
199. Hannah Leach, b. Jan. 29, 1813.
200. Seth Leach, b. Dec. 24, 1814.
201. Hosea Leach, b. Nov. 7, 1819.
202. Chloe Leach, b. Feb. 3, 1822.
203. John Leach, b. Jan. 1, 1824.
204. Kisiah Leach, b. Dec. 28, 1827.
205. Harriet Augusta Leach, b. Oct. 6, 1830.

Hosea Leach (179) d. May 26, 1843.
Hannah K. Leach d. April 14, 1832.

MEHITABEL LEACH (180), dau. of Giles and Mehitabel Wilbur Leach, m. Samuel Chesman, Oct. 8, 1806.
Mehitabel Leach (180) died Sept. 26, 1857, at Salem, Col.
Co., Ohio. Samuel Chesman died Sept. 9, 1826, at Merrimac, N. H. Children:

206. Elvira Chesman, b. Sept. 9, 1807.
207. Julia Ann Chesman, b. Oct. 16, 1809.
208. Samuel Chesman, b. June 16, 1812.
209. Robert McGow Chesman, b. Jan. 19, 1820.

ABIGAIL LEACH (182), m. Elias Ware, of Wrentham, 1809. Children:

Their names unknown.

KESIAH LEACH (183), dau. of Giles and Mehitabel
Wilbur Leach, m. Lewis Bartlett. Children:

210. Hiram Bartlett.

211. Cordelia Bartlett.
212. Henry Watson Bartlett.

Kesiah Leach Bartlett (183) died 1823.

LEWIS BARTLETT, m. Laura Leach Richmond, dau. of Giles and Mehitabel Wilbur Leach. Children.

213. Naham Bartlett, d.
214. John Bartlett, d. 1894.
215. Kiziah Bartlett, d. 1891.
216. Mary J. Bartlett.

Prior to the marriage of Laura (184) to Lewis Bartlett she had married a man by the name of Richmond, by whom she had two daughters:

217. Laura Richmond.
218. Kisiah Lucy Richmond.

LAURA RICHMOND (217), m. Benjamin Hayward Washburn, son of Olive and Mary Hayward Washburn, of W. Bridgewater, b. in 1806.

KESIAH LUCY RICHMOND (218), m. Asa Nye Bodfish. Children:

219. A son, b. Dec., 1852.

MARY J. BARTLETT (216), m. William White Cross, son of Nathaniel Henry and Lucy Vose Cross, b. Nov. 20, 1833. Child:

220. William Cross, Jr., b. Nov., 1858.

BETSEY LEACH (185), dau. of Giles and Mehitabel
Wilbur Leach, m. Jarvis Manly, of Boston, Mass. Children:

    221. William R. Manly, b. ——: d. in Tenn. in 1859,
        unmarried.
    222. Ruth E. Manly, b. in Easton, Mass., Nov., 1825.
    223. Rebecca B. Manly, b. in Canton, Mass., March 12.
        1831; she d. March 22, 1896, at Harrisburg, Pa.

RUTH E. MANLY (222), m. Henry Heylman. Children:

    224. A daughter, Anna Rebecca Heylman, b. July 14.
        1852; m. Charles Heylman, Oct. 9, 1873. No
        child.

REBECCA B. MANLEY (223), m. Rev. Benjamin
Hamlin, of Pa. Children:

    225. Benjamin R. Hamlin.
    226. Nancy H. Hamlin.
    227. Arma H. Hamlin.

Jarvis Hamlin died in 1872. His wife in 1862. Both
72 years of age.

GILES LEACH (187), son of Giles and Mehitabel Wilbur Leach, m. Lucy K. French, dau. of the Hon. Samuel
French, of Berkley, Jan. 20, 1820. Children:

    228. Lucy Caroline Leach, b. Nov. 12, 1821.
    229. Giles Luther Leach, b. July 10, 1823.

230. Elvira Chessman Leach, b. June 27, 1825.

231. Carolan Leach, b. Dec. 27, 1827; d. Dec. 30, 1892.

232. Valeria C. Leach, b. July 21, 1832; d. April 6, 1850.

233. Emily Adelaid Leach, b. June 29, 1841; d. Jan. 3, 1888.

234. Alice Leach, b. Aug. 7, 1844; d. Dec. 24, 1851.

HON. GILES LUTHER LEACH (229), son of Giles and Lucy K. French Leach, m., June 17, 1857. Hertilla Sawyer, of Standish, or Dighton, Mass. She d. March 25, 1858. He m. Betsey Toby Sprague Hathaway, of Berkley, Feb. 13, 1861. Children:

235. Harry Sprague Leach, b. March 5, 1863.

236. Carrie Toby Leach, b. Dec. 9, 1866.

237. Giles Edward Leach, b. June 2, 1868.

238. Jesse Porter Leach, b. Oct. 31, 1872.

LUCY CAROLINE LEACH (228), dau. of Giles and Lucy K. French Leach, m. Pythagorus Dean, Nov. 14, 1841. Children:

239. Caroline B. Dean, b. March 23, 1843.

240. Helen Mariah Dean, b. May 7, 1845.

241. George Ferdinand Dean, b. Aug. 19, 1847.

Helen M. Dean d. April 2, 1848.
George F. Dean d. Sept. 1, 1848.
Pythagoras Dean d. Feb. 24, 1869.

Lucy C. Leach Dean then m. W. H. Viles, March 20, 1870. W. H. Viles d. April 12, 1872. Lucy C. (228) m.

Jonathan Avery Pratt, June 15, 1875. Jonathan A. Pratt d. Feb. 1, 1886. Lucy C. (228) d. Sept., 1897.

CAROLINE B. DEAN (239), dau. of Pythagoras and Lucy C. Leach Dean, m. Melvin Wilbur, son of Emory Stetson Wilbur, May 27, 1860. Children:

242. Francis Vernon Wilbur, b. Oct. 15, 1861.
243. Erminie Dean Wilbur, b. Aug. 11, 1866.
244. Lillian Richmond Wilbur. b. Sept. 20, 1871.

Francis Vernon Wilbur d. May 11, 1863.
Erminie D. Wilbur (243) m. William Mason King. May 25, 1893.

On the following pages will be found a record of the descendants of Mehitabel Leach (180), dau. of Giles and Mehitabel Wilbur Leach:

ELVIRA CHESMAN (206), dau. of Mehitabel Leach and Samuel Chesman, m. Jonathan M. Jackman, Aug. 22 1829. Children:

245. Samuel Stillman Jackman, b. Dec. 30, 1830.
246. John Henry Jackman, b. Dec. 19, 1832.
247. Richard Pattee Jackman, b. Dec. 16, 1834.
248. Charles Bradley Jackman, b. May 30, 1837.
249. George Little Jackman, b. Dec. 26, 1839.
250. Sarah Betsey Jackman, b. Oct. 14, 1841.
251. Lemuel Noyes Jackman, b. Feb. 21, 1843.
252. Frank Edward Jackman, b. March 6, 1845.
253. Abby Francena Jackman, b. Dec. 17, 1848.

JULIA ANN CHESMAN (207), dau. of Mehitabel Leach and Samuel Chesman, m. Elva E. Bradley, of Woodstock, Vt. They had five daus., three of them d. young:

254. Emiline Elvira Bradley, b. Sept. 22, 1830.
255. Frances Bradley, b. Jan. 20, 1832.

Bradley d. in April, 1837, and Julia m. John Otterson, of Allegheny Co., Pa., in Jan., 1838. Children:

256. Julia Ann Otterson, b. March 2, 1840.
257. John Otterson, b. Jan. 19, 1842.
258. Robert Otterson, b. Jan. 19. 1844.
259. Samuel Otterson, b. Nov., 1846; d. young.

SAMUEL CHESMAN (208), son of Mehitabel Leach and Samuel Chesman. m. Jane Gorden, dau. of John and Jane McClintock Gorden, of Plumb Township, Allegheny Co., Pa., March 27, 1834. Children:

260. Henry Warren Chessman, b. March 13, 1835.
261. Elvira Jane Chessman, b. July 16, 1839.
262. Mary Ann Chessman, b. Oct. 16, 1842.
263. Martha Chessman, b. May 3, 1847.
264. Lewis Gorden Chessman, b. April 28, 1854; d. Oct. 15, 1852.
265. George Gorden Chessman, b. July 22, 1853.

ROBERT McGAW CHESMAN (209). son of Mehitabel Leach and Samuel Chesman. m. Maria Stewart, dau. of David and Barbara Miller Stewart, of Allegheny Co., Pa. Children:

Six died young.

266. Harriet Ann Chessman, b. Nov. 10, 1839.

267. Samuel Melvin Chessman, b. Dec. 23. 1848.

268. Orin Austin Chessman. b. Aug. 16, 1853.

Maria, the first wife, died.   Robert m. Mary Ross Morton, dau. of John and Nancy Morton, of Pittsburg, Pa. Children:

269. Ewart Morton Chessman, b. June 16, 1859.

270. George Haney Chessman. b. March 28, 1861.

271. Otis Stewart Chessman, b. Oct. 21, 1864.

SAMUEL STILLMAN JACKMAN (245), grandson of Mehitabel Leach Chessman, m. Lydia Ann Balcom. One child:

272. Ella Frances Jackman, b. Oct. 21, 1857.

Ella m. Frank O. Ray, March 24, 1875.

JOHN HENRY JACKMAN (246), grandson of Mehitabel Leach Chessman, m. Eliza F. Riddle, Oct. 11, 1860. One child:

273. James H. Jackman, b. Aug. 31. 1861; m. Stella F. Mason, Jan. 3, 1882.

RICHARD PATTEE JACKMAN (247), grandson of Mehitabel Leach Chessman. m. Samantha Clark, May 23. 1857. Two children:

274. George Little Jackman, b. Nov. 28, 1860.

275. Isabel Etta Jackman, b. May 10, 1867; m. Robert W. Joslyn, Aug. 8. 1888.   Children:

276. George Robert Joslyn, b. Oct. 7, 1890.
277. Homer L. Joslyn, b. Aug. 25, 1892.
Residence, Elgin, Ill.

CHARLES BRADLEY JACKMAN (248), grandson
of Mehitabel Leach Chessman, m. Eliza Humphrey, Aug.
15, 1861. Children:

278. Charles Humphrey Jackman, b. July 16, 1862.
279. Clara Francena Jackman, b. Feb. 1, 1869.

Charles Humphrey Jackman (278) m. Mertie Wilson.
Sept. 13, 1885.

GEORGE LITTLE JACKMAN (249), grandson of
Mehitabel Leach Chessman, m. Lucinda Averil Thompson, Nov. 25, 1862. Children:

280. Alice Lucinda Jackman, b. Aug. 18, 1863.
281. Flora Elvira Jackman, b. Feb. 6, 1872.

Flora Elvira Jackman d. Dec. 16, 1891.

SARAH BETSEY JACKMAN (250), granddaughter
of Mehitabel Leach Chessman, m. John Moulton Adams,
June 27, 1863. No children.

LEMUEL NOYES JACKMAN (251), grandson of
Mehitabel Leach Chessman, m. Georgie H. Park. Two
children, d. young. She d. May 30, 1869. He m., 2d
wife, Louise A. Otis, Dec. 20, 1871. One child:

282. Ida Louisa Jackman, b. May 28, 1874.

FRANK EDWARD JACKMAN (252), grandson of Mehitabel Leach Chessman, m. Sarah S. Hall, Oct. 9, 1870. Children:

283. Nellie Elvira Jackman, b. Nov. 10, 1871. Nellie died young.
284. Tena May Jackman, b. June 8, 1874.
285. Eugene Layton Jackman, b. Nov. 24, 1875.
286. Lizzie Geraldine Jackman, b. Dec. 28, 1888.

ABBY FRANCENA JACKMAN (253), granddaughter of Mehitabel Leach Chessman, m. George Messer, July 12, 1871. One child that died young. Messer died. She then m. Daniel W. Hancock, May 13, 1882.

EMELINE ELVIRA BRADLEY (254), granddaughter of Mehitabel Leach Chessman, m. William Garberick, of Harrisburg, Pa., in 1851. Two children that died young.

FRANCES BRADLEY (255), granddaughter of Mehitabel Leach Chessman, m. Otis Young, in 1852. One daughter:

290. Laura B. Young, b. Jan. 31, 1854.

JULIA ANN OTTERSON (256), granddaughter of Mehitabel Leach Chessman, m. John Cook Dyson, June 1, 1858. Children:

291. Clara Julia Dyson, b. Oct. 14, 1861; d. in 1874.
292. Frank Jackman Dyson, b. Feb. 21, 1867.

293. Samuel Chessman Dyson, b. Feb. 15, 1869. Samuel C. Dyson was killed on the railroad Dec., 1895.
294. John Charles Dyson, b. Jan. 25, 1871.
295. Otis Young Dyson, b. Dec. 20. 1872.
296. Robert Otterson Dyson, b. Nov. 16, 1874.

HENRY WARREN CHESSMAN (260), grandson of Mehitabel Leach Chessman, m. Lavina Sharp, of Salem, Ohio, March 8, 1860. She died March 18, 1862. He died June 6, 1868. No children. Warren was a soldier in the 115th Regt. O. Vols. during its nearly three years' service.

ELVIRA JANE CHESSMAN (261), granddaughter of Mehitabel Leach Chessman, m. Jonathan R. Oliphant, Feb. 26, 1863. Children:

297. Harry Grant Oliphant, b. Oct. 2, 1865.
298. Lavina Elizabeth Oliphant, b. Oct. 10, 1867.
Two children died young.

Harry Grant Oliphant (294) m. Agnes Mary Button, of Bridgeport, Conn., dau. of Edward W. and Margaret Demster Button, Oct. 20, 1891. Born to them:

299. Margaret Sayers Oliphant, b. Aug. 18, 1893.

MARY ANN CHESSMAN (262), granddaughter of Mehitabel Leach Chessman, m. Hiram Taylor, of Mahoning Co., Ohio, April 14, 1881. No children.

MARTHA CHESSMAN (263) granddaughter of Mehitabel Leach Chessman, m. Augustus H. Harris, of Salem, Ohio. Oct. 13, 1868.   Children:

   300. Warren Henry Harris, b. June 20, 1871.
   301. Helen Harris, b. Sept. 16, 1885; m. Jean, dau. of Jonathan K. and Katharine Rukenbrod, of Salem, Ohio, June 4, 1895.

GEORGE GORDEN CHESSMAN (265), grandson of Mehitabel Leach Chessman, m. Jennie L. Wharton, Feb. 25, 1875.   Children:

One died young.
   302. Linnie Chessman, b. Sept. 1, 1882.

Jennie L. Chessman died.   George then m., for 2d wife, Mattie Morris, of Mahoning Co., Ohio, Feb. 21, 1892. Born to them:

   303. Samuel Morris Chessman, b. March 3, 1894; d. Aug. 5, 1894.

HARRIET ANN CHESSMAN (266), granddaughter of Mehitabel Leach Chessman, m. Alexander Smith.   Ten children:

   304. Robert Chessman Smith, b. Jan. 14, 1859.
   305. Charles Alexander Smith, b. Oct. 15, 1865.
   306. Mary Ella Smith, b. Feb. 1, 1868.
   307. Ann Luella Smith, b. March 23, 1870.
   308. Olie Wendal Smith, b. Dec. 31, 1874.
   309. George William Smith, b. July 2, 1878.
Four children died young.

SAMUEL MELVIN CHESSMAN (267), grandson of Mehitabel Leach Chessman, m. Matilda Brawdy, June 9, 1870. Ten children:

Six died young.
310. Ora Xenic Chessman, b. April 22, 1871.
311. Nannie Luella Chessman, b. Aug. 23, 1877.
312. Robert Brawdy Chessman, b. May 16, 1875.
313. Eva Frances Chessman, b. June 2, 1886.

Ora Xenia Chessman (310) m. Albert Deshler, June 29, 1893. By the Rev. T. M. Thompson.
Nannie Luella Chessman (311) m. Clyde Van Asdale. 1895.

ORIN AUSTIN CHESSMAN (268), grandson of Mehitabel Leach Chessman, m. Jennie E. Maxwell, Sept. 19, 1872. Children:

314. Samuel Covert Chessman, b. Aug. 14, 1873.
315. Emma May Chessman, b. Dec. 14, 1875.
316. Harriet Elmira Chessman, b. Nov. 10, 1880.

EWART MORTON CHESSMAN (269), grandson of Mehitabel Leach Chessman, m. Ida M. Luther, June 2, 1893. One child:

317. Rachel Chessman, b. Nov., 1883; d. young.

GEORGE HANEY CHESSMAN (270), grandson of Mehitabel Leach Chessman, m. Lillie G. Hodgins. Feb. 26, 1883. One son:

318. George Wilbert Chessman, b. Feb. 22, 1885.

OTIS STEWART CHESSMAN (271), grandson of Mehitabel Leach Chessman, m. Annette Nichols, of Boston, Mass., June 25, 1889. One daughter:

319. Ethel Nichols Chessman, b. Jan. 5, 1893.

BENJAMIN LEACH (98), son of Dea. Joseph and Ann Harris Leach, m. Mary, dau. of Ebenezer Keith, 1764. Children:

320. Joseph Leach.
321. Luke Leach.
322. Silas Leach.
323. Japtha Leach.
324. Josiah Leach.
325. Mary Leach.
326. Orphah Leach.
327. Lois Leach.
328. Hepzibah Leach.
329. Dinah Leach.

The wife, Ann, died 1791. He m. Anna Short, 1792. Children:

330. Anna Leach, b. 1793.
331. Eunice Leach, b. 1796.
332. Chloe Leach, b. 1799.

Mary Leach (325) m. Libeus Fobs. Jr., 1807.
Orpha Leach (326) m. Jacob Chipman.
Lois Leach (327) m. James Star, Esq., 1797.
Hepzibah Leach (328) m. Marshall Keith, 1798.

Dinah Leach (329) m. Fiske Ames, 1819.
Anna Leach (330) m. Galen Harvey, 1817.
Eunice Leach (331) m. Otis Harvey, 1819.

JEDEDIAH LEACH (101), son of Benjamin and Hannah Keith Leach, m. Phebe, dau. of Robert Keith, 1765. Children:

 333. Wealthy Leach, b. 1767.
 334. Bernice Leach, b. 1767.

 Phebe, the wife, d. 1811. Jedediah d. 1813.
 Wealthy Leach (338) m. Joseph Leach, 1788.
 Bernice Leach (334) m. Roxana, dau. of Nathaniel Hooper, 1797. For 2d wife Bernice m. Olive, dau. of William Keith, 1810.

LEMUEL LEACH (109), son of Stephen and Lydia Flora Leach, m. Rebecca, dau. of William Washburn, 1767. Children:

 335. Oliver Leach, b. 1768.

They removed to Hardwick and then to Wendell. Had eight more children:

 336. Lemuel Leach.
 337. Stephen Leach.
 338. Gardner Leach.
 339. Barnabas Leach.
 340. Lewis Leach.
 341. Artemas Leach.

342. Matilda Leach.

343. Rebecca Leach.

Gardner Leach (338) was representative in 1839.

CAPT. LOT LEACH (112), son of Capt. Simon and Elizabeth Curtis Leach, m. A. Keith. Children:

344. Simon Leach.

345. Betsey Leach, m. Perez Southworth, Jr., 1821.

EBENEZER LEACH (118), son of Daniel and Pethiah Leach, m. Eunice, dau. of Benjamin Keith. He died in 1834.

LEVI LEACH (132), son of Jonathan and Abigail Leach, m. Betsey, dau. of Zenus Conant, 1798. Children:

346. Deborah Jackson Leach, b. 1799.

347. Giles Leach, b. 1801.

348. Anna Leach, b. 1807.

349. Clarinda Leach, b. 1810.

350. Betsy Leach, b. 1812.

351. Sarah Leach, b. 1816.

352. Levi Leach, b. 1818.

353. George M. Leach, b. 1821.

Giles Leach (347), son of Jonathan and Abigail Conant Leach, graduated at Brown University.

ALPHEUS LEACH (155), son of James and Huzadiah Keith Leach, m. Cassandra, dau. of William Keith, 1787. Children:

354. Anna Leach, b. 1787.
355. Ambrose Leach, b. 1791.
356. Sally Leach, b. 1793.
357. Alpheus Leach, b. 1796.
358. Louisa Leach, b. 1800.
359. Wightman Rathburn Leach, b. 1800.
360. Hepzibah Rathburn Leach, b. 1806.
361. James Keith Leach, b. 1811.

AMBROSE LEACH (355), son of Alpheus and Huzadiah Keith Leach, m. Hannah, dau. of Nehemiah Howard, 1815.

ALPHEUS LEACH (357), son of Alpheus and Huzadiah Keith Leach, m. Eliza, dau. of Bradford Mitchel.

APOLLOS LEACH (156), son of James Leach, m. Chloe, dau. of Christopher Dyer. Children:

362. Philo Leach, b. 1797.
363. Sarah Leach, b. 1801.
364. Oliver Leach, b. 1803.
365. Daniel Leach, b. 1806.
366. Franklin Leach, b. 1809.
367. Philander Leach, b. 1813.

Daniel Leach (365) graduated at Brown University in 1830; m. Mary Lawton, of Newport, and lived in Quincy, and afterwards in Roxbury.

Franklin Leach (366) m. dau. of Isaac Fobes.

Sarah Leach (363) m. Ansel Perkins, of North Bridgewater.

WILLIAM LEACH (parentage not known). m. Mary Cahoon in 1741. Children:

> 368. Jonathan Leach, b. 1742.
> 369. Olive Leach, b. 1747.
> 370. Deborah Leach, b. 1750.
> 371. Hepzibah Leach, b. 1752.
> 372. Catharine Leach, b. 1756.

Deborah Leach (370) m. Nathan Leach (67), son of Timothy and Sarah Leach, 1771.

ZADOCK LEACH (175), son of Zadock and Susanna Washburn Leach, m. Polly Frost, of West Cambridge. Children:

> 373. Jane Leach.
> 374. Vesta Leach.
> 375. Betsey Leach.
> 376. Zadock Washburn Leach.

Jane Leach (373) m. a Mr. Hammond, of Rochester.

ABRAHAM LEACH (171), son of Zadock and Susanna Washburn Leach, m. Mary, dau. of Amos Keith, 1796. Children:

> 377. Eliza Leach.
> 378. Libeus Leach.
> 379. Susanna Leach.
> 380. Jesse Leach.
> 381. Eveline Leach.

Abraham Leach (171) went to N. Y. and died.

Eliza Leach (377) m. Cyrus Miller, of Northfield.

Libeus Leach (378) m. Mary Brooks, of West Cambridge.

Susanna Leach (379) m. Wm., son of Ivins Grant.

Jesse Leach (380) m. Mary Ann Miller and settled in N. Y.

BOZER LEACH (170), son of Zadock and Susanna Washburn Leach, m. Betsey Shaw, of M., 1793. Children:

382. Ezra Leach.

383. Isaac Leach.

384. Anne Leach.

JOSEPH LEACH (317), son of Benjamin and Ann Harris Leach, m. Wealthy, dau. of Jedediah Leach, 1788. Children:

385. Clarissa Leach, who m. Ezekiel Dyer, 1811.

LUKE LEACH (318), son of Benjamin and Mary Keith Leach, m. Polly Star, 1788.   Children:

386. Amory Leach.

387. Harris Leach.

Luke Leach removed to Me.

Amory Leach (386) m. Lydia, dau. of Job Bearce, 1817.

SILAS LEACH (322), son of Benjamin and Mary Keith Leach, m. Lois Leach (130), 1796, and went to S. Carolina.

THOMAS LEACH, son of Seth.   Children:

388. Thomas Leach.
389. Ebenezer Leach.
390. Seth Leach.
And several daughters.

Sarah Leach m. Dea. John Soule, 1807.
Seth Leach (387) m. Mercy Sampson, of M., 1819.
Thomas Leach (388) m. Mary Nasbit, of Leeds, 1809,
and Susan Holbrook, of Braintree, in 1814.

ELIPHLET LEACH (138), son of Nathan and Deborah Leach, m. Hannah Shaw, dau. of Asa Shaw, 1806.
Children:

391. Isaac Leach, b. 1807.
392. Nahum Leach, b. 1809.
393. Hannah Leach, b.
394. Washington Leach, b. 1812.
395. Dexter Leach, b. 1814.
396. Martha Leach, b. 1815.

NATHAN LEACH (139), son of Nathan and Deborah
Leach, m. Mehitabel Gloyd.   Children:

397. Nathan Leach, b. 1805.
398. George Washington Leach, b. 1807.
399. Mehitabel Leach, b. 1809.
400. Eliza Leach, b. 1811.
401. Sally Leach, b. 1814.

PELEG LEACH (parentage not known), m. Sally Gilmore, 1802. Children:

402. Peleg Leach, b. 1802.
403. Sarah Field Leach, b. 1804.
404. Adaline Conant Leach, b. 1806.
405. Olive Leach, b. 1807.
406. Elisha Gilmore Leach, b. 1809.
407. William Terrill Leach, b. 1810.
408. Ebenezer Leach, b. 1813.

PHILO LEACH, ESQ. (362), son of Apollos and Huzadiah Leach, m. Lucia, dau. of Capt. Joseph Hooper. One son:

409. James Edward Leach, b. 1825.

MARY ANN LEACH (197), dau. of Hosea and Hannah Keith Leach, m. John Hall, Dec. 25, 1831. Children:

410. Mary Ann Hall.

John Hall died. She m. Harvey Kimball. One child:

411. Alice Kimball, died.

LAMBERT LEACH (198), son of Hosea and Hannah Keith Leach, m. Lydia Sherman in 1835. They had three sons and two daus., names not known.

HANNAH LEACH (199), dau. of Hosea and Hannah Keith Leach, m. Marcus Conant, May 17, 1835. Children:

412. Phebe Conant, b. Sept. 21, 1836 (b. in Bridgewater).

413. Joanna Conant, b. April 25, 1890; m. Alfred Hall.

PHEBE CONANT (412), dau. of Marcus and Hannah
Conant, and granddaughter of Hosea and Hannah Keith
Leach, m. James Cushing Leach, of Bridgewater, 1860.
Children:

414. Jason Leach, b. July 25, 1865; d. young.

415. Albert Marcus Leach, b. Nov. 18, 1871.

416. Harriet Augusta Leach, b. Jan., 1863; d. young.

Albert Marcus died Aug. 24, 1872.

James Cushing Leach was the son of Alpheus Leach, of
Bridgewater, b. June 11, 1831; d. Oct. 3, 1895. During
his life he held many offices of trust. He represented his
town in the State senate. At his funeral he was honored
by the attendance of twenty-three State senators and the
sergeant-at-arms, and a large delegation of Masons and
bank officers.

KIZIAH LEACH (204), dau. of Hosea and Hannah
Keith Leach, m. Warren Sampson. Children:

417. Everet.

418. Edith.

419. Caroline.

420. Willie.

CHLOE LEACH, dau. of Hosea and Hannah Keith
Leach, m. Nehemiah White. One daughter:

421. ————.

SETH LEACH (200), son of Hosea and Hannah Keith
Leach, m. a Diffenback.

HOSEA LEACH (201), son of Hosea and Hannah
Leach, m. Elizabeth ————.

HANNAH LEACH CONANT (199), dau. of Hosea
and Hannah Kieth Leach, died May 8, 1889, of cancer.

JOANNA CONANT (413), dau. of Marcus and Hannah Leach Conant, m. Alfred Hall, Aug. 8, 1864. Children:

422. Phebe Maria Hall, b. May 29, 1865; d. March 4.
1870.
423. Francis Marcus Hall, ⎫
424. William Martin Hall, ⎬ twins, b. Jan. 17, 1881.